SHONEN JUMP'S

ONE PIECE™

The CIRCUS COMES to TOWN

Adapted by Howie Dewin

SCHOLASTIC INC.

New York   Toronto   London   Auckland   Sydney
Mexico City   New Delhi   Hong Kong   Buenos Aires

No part of this publication may be reproduced, stored in a retrieval system, or transmitted in any form or by any means, electronic, mechanical, photocopying, recording, or otherwise, without written permission of the publisher. For information regarding permission, write to Scholastic Inc., Attention: Permissions Department, 557 Broadway, New York, NY 10012.

ISBN-10: 0-439-89726-2
ISBN-13: 978-0-439-89726-6

© 2006 Eiichiro Oda / Shueisha, Toei Animation

Published by Scholastic Inc.
SCHOLASTIC and associated logos are trademarks and/or registered trademarks of Scholastic Inc.

12 11 10 9 8 7 6 5 4 3 2 1   6 7 8 9 10 11/0

Designed by Phil Falco
Printed in the U.S.A.
First printing, November 2006

PROLOGUE

There once was a man named Gold Roger, who was the King of the Pirates. He had fame, power, and wealth beyond your wildest dreams.

Before they hung him from the gallows, these were the final words he said, "My fortune is yours for the taking but you'll have to find it first. I've left everything in One Piece."

Ever since, men and women from all over the world set sail for the Grand Line, searching for One Piece, the treasure that would make their dreams come true.

CHAPTER ONE

Adrift in Memory

Way out on the high seas where the blue of the sky stretches on forever, an enormous clipper ship cut cleanly through the salt waters. Atop the ship flew a flag emblazoned with the image of a skull and crossbones. Any innocent passerby would not have had the slightest doubt that this ship was up to no good. But something about that skull and crossbones was not quite right. Directly in the center of its bony face was a large, red, round clown nose. Any pirate worth his salt knew what that meant — this vessel was under the command of the ruthless Cap'n Buggy!

Standing at the center of the main deck, three unkempt and nasty-looking pirates hunched over a large trunk. Their cruel laughter rang out over the waters as they pulled glittering gems from the trunk, allowing the gems to dangle in the sunlight and letting strands of the priceless jewels spill from their grasp.

"Aye! Cap'n Buggy will be mighty pleased with this swag!" they chortled.

Just then, something in the distance caught the eye of one of the dirty scoundrels. "Hey, look mateys, portside!" He pointed off in the distance to a small sailboat, much smaller than the pirate's vessel. "Sail ho! Let's make a raid!"

They brought their ship up alongside the smaller boat. A young girl was draped over the side of the boat, her arm slapping the surface of the water. Her short red hair fell over her face. She did not move.

"I dunno, me hearties. Looks like someone may have beat us to it," said one of the pirates.

"Are you alive, lassie?" prodded the first pirate.

Much to their surprise, the young girl lifted her head. Her eyes opened wide in amazement. "Oh!" she said in a honey-sweet voice. "Am I dreaming or have I been rescued by men who are even more handsome than I could have imagined?"

The pirates laughed. Such a sweet young girl would be easy prey!

"Could you spare some water?" asked the girl, sweat falling off her face. "Perhaps a piece of bread?" Then she gestured to a bejeweled trunk behind her. "If you want gold, take it. But please, help me."

"Of course! It'd be our plunder — er, I mean, *pleasure!*" said the pirate leading the other two aboard the little boat.

"Yes! Our treasure! Er . . . *pleasure!*" echoed another.

The three greedy pirates bent over the chest, forgetting about the young girl. They heard nothing but the gentle lapping of the water against the little skiff and the sound of their own evil laughter as they quickly broke through the ruby-studded clasp meant

3

to safekeep the contents of the trunk. In no time they were lifting the lid.

"Let's have a look!" They cackled.

BOING! A huge panda head on an enormous coil sprang from the trunk and towered menacingly over the pirates!

AAUUGGHH!! The pirates leapt back, confused and frightened.

Before they could even begin to realize how they'd been tricked, the sweet young girl was calling out to them from a distance.

"Take the whole boat while you're at it!" she yelled. "It's all yours!"

As they turned to grab her, they saw the red-haired girl standing on the deck of their ship as it sailed quickly away from them.

"She took our ship!" one of the pirates cried.

"Looks like clouds coming in low from the south," she called out, "which means a cold front, folks. Small vessels should take precautions against capsizing!"

She couldn't help laughing. The pirates got exactly what they deserved! Before she could say another word, dark clouds rolled in and rain began to pummel the small boat. In no time, the boat and its three pirate passengers sunk!

"Bingo!" she cried out. "So long!"

*   *   *

Meanwhile, in another part of the ocean blue, an even smaller boat drifted aimlessly.

"Boy, I'm starving," said a teenage boy leaning against one side of the tiny boat. His hair was jet-black and covered by an old straw hat with a red tie.

Leaning against the other side of the boat was a strong young man with green hair. "Me too!" he agreed. "When are we going to reach shore, Luffy?" It was clear from his tone he was growing tired and angry. "It's kinda strange for someone trying to be King of the Pirates not to know how to navigate!"

"Drifting has always worked pretty well for me before," Luffy answered, too tired to lift his head. "But how about you, Zolo," he shot back. "You're supposed to be the terror of the seas!"

"Once I went hunting for a pirate and got stranded in the ocean. So I made the best of things.

I always went after pirates that were nearby — I had to earn cash somehow," the green-haired hero responded.

"Right," Luffy spat back at Zolo, "so you got lost too!"

"Hey!" Zolo shouted as he lurched toward Luffy, "you don't have to put it like that!"

His sudden burst of temper shifted the balance in the little boat. It rocked chaotically back and forth. Luffy was tossed to the floor. His hat was knocked off his head and then caught in an updraft. In a split second, his hat was high above him, well out of reach.

"Oh, no!" he cried. "My straw hat!"

Suddenly Luffy was lost in memory. He heard the voice of Shanks, a man from deep in his past, as he watched his hat dance in the wind along the top of the sail.

"Luffy m'lad," the red-haired Shanks said to the little boy who lived in Luffy's memory. "This lucky hat has been through many a battle with me. It's so precious, in fact, I can't ever part with it!" Shanks tossed the straw hat again and again into the air.

"I can't lose it!" Luffy cried in desperation, ripping himself from the memory. "You don't know what that hat means to me!"

Zolo and Luffy raced to the bow of the boat. The hat fell away from the updraft. It began to weave its way down, zigzagging toward the water. Zolo leaned far out over the water, his fingers stretching toward the hat. Luffy watched in terror as memory overtook him.

In his mind's eye, he was a young boy surrounded by boisterous pirates in an old seaport saloon. Perched on a bar stool, he sat next to the red-headed pirate named Shanks. It was Shanks who had given him his hat. It was Shanks who had made him promise to one day return the hat.

As Luffy's eyes desperately followed the erratic movement of the straw hat as it made its way to the water to be lost forever, he could hear Shanks' voice like he was whispering right in his ear.

"Ya must promise to give it back someday. When you've become a great pirate . . ."

CHAPTER TWO

The Passing of the Hat

"Har, har, har!"

"Another round on me!"

"More! More! More!"

The saloon was jammed with rowdy pirates, shout-ing and singing, laughing and drinking. They stuffed their faces with food and swigged beer from great mugs. They were rude and loud and the little boy at the bar could think of nowhere he'd rather be. To be a pirate was the finest dream a boy could have — especially a pirate like Shanks, who had just told him another great story from the seas.

"You and that hat have had some great adventures, Shanks! Take me with you on your next journey!" little Luffy cried.

"You, on our next journey?" Shanks said, brushing his red hair back under his hat and laughing at the small boy. "Ha!"

The other pirates joined in the laughter.

"Just 'cause you're a good swimmer doesn't mean you'd be a good pirate!" Yasopp the pirate said.

Luffy was infuriated. How dare they not take him seriously! "But I got a punch like a rocket!" he shouted, his arm jabbing at air to prove his point.

"Sure you do," Shanks smiled.

"What's that mean?!" demanded Luffy, enraged at being treated like a kid.

"It means you're a boy, mate!"

"I am not! I'm a man!"

Shanks nodded. "Keep yer air! Have some apple juice."

Luffy jumped at the offer. "Wow! Thanks!"

Shanks laughed, "That proves me point, Luffy! A man would never drink apple juice!"

Luffy slammed down the mug. He couldn't believe he'd been tricked. But before he could protest too loudly, the swinging doors of the saloon burst open, one actually flying from its hinges.

"Make way for the Scourge of the Mountains!" boomed Higuma, a towering mass of a man. His hair in a topknot, he was surrounded by a group of angry bandanna-wearing bandits. He quickly studied the now silent men scattered about the saloon.

"So these are pirates, huh?" he sneered. "Looks like a sorry lot to me!"

Shanks kept his head low but watched Higuma closely. Luffy watched Shanks.

"Can I help you gentlemen?" Makino, the barmaid, asked calmly.

"We're mountain bandits," Higuma snarled. "But relax, we're not gonna bust the place up. We just want ten hogsheads of somethin' strong!"

"But we don't have any strong stuff left," Makino said.

"So what are all these pirates drinking?" he barked.

"Sorry about that," Shanks broke in. "Guess we drank it all up!" He reached down and picked up one unopened bottle. "But here, why don't ya have this? It hasn't even been opened yet."

In the blink of an eye, Higuma's rage ignited. With one powerful blow of his fist, he shattered the bottle in Shanks' outstretched hand.

"You fool!" Higuma bellowed. "What kind of man do you take me for? One bottle means nothing! You understand?"

Shanks, dripping wet, knelt down to the floor to pick up the shards of glass. "What a mess," he muttered to Makino. "I'll clean it up."

"No, I'll get it," she replied quietly.

Luffy watched in amazement. Why wasn't Shanks defending his honor?

Higuma towered over him. He drew his sword and cleared the entire contents of the bar onto Shanks' head. "I'm a wanted man with eight million berries on my head. I've done away with fifty-six men! Mostly cowards like you! You should consider yourself lucky I broke the glass and not your skull."

Higuma strode out of the bar, followed by his band of troublemakers. Makino knelt at Shanks' side.

"Captain Shanks," she said. "You're totally soaked!"

The pirates remained silent, waiting to hear if Shanks could speak.

"I'm sorry," Makino said, truly upset.

"Don't be," Shanks muttered slowly and quietly, his face still hidden by the lowered brim of his hat. "Some of it got in me mouth!"

Shanks burst into laughter. The crew of pirates followed his lead and exploded with laughter too.

"Some of it got in his mouth!" Yasopp echoed in laughter.

"You think it's funny?" Little Luffy shouted. "He made you look like a weakling! Why didn't you fight him? What kind of pirate takes those insults?"

"Luffy," Shanks smiled. "You have to pick your battles! Now how 'bout eatin' some grub?"

"I'm not hungry!" he shouted and turned away.

But then he looked down to see one of Shanks' treasure chests open. Inside was a large purple fruit.

I may not be hungry, *thought Luffy*, but that fruit does look pretty tasty. *No one was looking as Luffy grabbed a piece of the fruit. Shanks was still laughing when he looked over and spied the young boy shoving the fruit into his mouth.*

"Luffy!" Shanks cried, springing to his feet. "Tell me ya didn't eat that purple piece of fruit!"

"But I did," Luffy declared.

Shanks grabbed the boy and turned him upside down. "Throw up! Right now! Throw up everything you ate!" He shook the boy as hard as he could but nothing came up. Then, without warning, Shanks felt the boy's legs stretch like rubber beneath his hands. Then his neck stretched so far that his head hit the floor. Shanks knew it was too late.

"What just happened," Luffy asked slowly.

"You ate the cursed Gum Gum fruit, Luffy!" Shanks cried. "Which means you're just like rubber! And you'll never be able to swim for the rest of your life!"

Whether or not he was a rubber boy now, Luffy had

to settle the score. He couldn't stand thinking those mountain bandits thought they could treat pirates that way. He'd stand up to Higuma if no one else would! It didn't take long before Luffy was all alone facing Higuma and his men in the town square.

"Here's how I see it, punk!" Higuma spat as he threw Luffy to the ground. "Your little friends can't stand up for themselves so you stand up for them, is that it?"

"Don't make fun of Shanks!" Luffy demanded. "Take it back!"

"Shanks is a spineless coward," he roared.

"Apologize or else," Luffy shouted. Higuma's foot bore down on Luffy's head.

"Your sharp tongue is about to taste my sword!"

Just then, Makino arrived with the mayor of the town behind her.

"Wait!" the old mayor called out. "Stop! Let the boy go! I don't know what Luffy did but if it's money you want, you'll get it. Just please, don't hurt the boy!"

"Don't beg!" Luffy spat out. Even with Higuma's enormous foot weighing down on him, he couldn't stop fighting. It went against every bit of his pirate soul.

"Nice try, old man," Higuma laughed, "but it's too late for this brat!"

Makino and the mayor pleaded with Higuma as Luffy continued to insult him. Higuma raised his sword.

"Luffy!" cried Makino.

Just then, a familiar voice rose up. "It's the mountain bandits again!"

"Captain Shanks!" Makino cried in relief.

"Shanks!" Luffy called out as Higuma grunted in disgust.

"I thought your punch was as powerful as a rocket, Luffy!" Shanks said calmly, his crew behind him.

Higuma turned his attention to Shanks. "I warned ye — You can use yer head and leave, or stay and we'll use yer head for something else!"

Shanks didn't listen. He walked coolly toward Higuma and Luffy. But the cold barrel of a pistol was suddenly at his temple.

"Like target practice," snarled Higuma's man who held the pistol.

The pirates eyed the mountain bandits as the mountain bandits eyed the pirates. Shanks didn't bat an eye.

"You're puttin' me on," he said. "These weapons misfire at such close range."

BANG! The mountain bandit collapsed as one of Shanks' pirates put away his revolver. The mountain bandits instantly decried the injustice.

"That wasn't fair," shouted one after the other.

Shanks laughed. "We don't play by the rules. We're pirates!" He turned to Higuma. "You can pour drinks on me. I'll just laugh it off. But nobody hurts a mate of mine. Now for the last time, let the lad go!"

Luffy watched his hero through one wide eye. Higuma's massive boot was pressing down hard on the other.

Higuma bellowed, "Quite a speech! But you pirates can't stand up to the mountain bandits!"

That was the last thing he said before the chaos was unleashed. The mountain bandits charged with swords drawn. Shanks did nothing but stand his ground as his man, Benn, stepped forward.

"Cap'n," Benn said coolly, "I'll take care of this."

Moments later, using his long-nosed pistol as a baton, Benn had downed every one of the bandits.

"Wow!" Luffy muttered, but there was no time to

admire the pirates' work because in that same instant, Higuma raised his hand high above his head. In his hand was a round black object. He threw it to the ground.

"A smoke bomb!" Shanks cried.

Then everything went dark.

* * *

Higuma was still laughing at his ingenious escape by the time they were bobbing up and down in a small boat far out in the ocean. He held Luffy threateningly out over the open waters.

"Let me go!" Luffy shouted.

"I intend to, m'boy! Because you made me angry!"

With that, Higuma launched the boy out into the water as Luffy remembered the cursed fruit and the fact that he could no longer swim!

SPLASH!

Higuma roared with evil laughter as Luffy flailed about, struggling to keep his head above water. His laughter, in fact, kept him from realizing what was about to be unleashed behind him.

But Luffy knew. Even as he grabbed at the water, he could see the enormous sea monster that was rising up behind Higuma. The roar of the ocean in Luffy's ears buried the roar of the beast but nothing could block the horror of its opened jaws as they closed around Higuma and swallowed the bandit and boat whole.

"Help me!" Luffy screamed in terror, "I can't swim!"

Suddenly the serpent was careening toward him with jaws opened. It was hard to know what happened next as the serpent bore down on him and the waves pulled him under. But in the next instant, there was Shanks facing down the serpent and taking control of the seas.

Another moment and Luffy was safe with Shanks.

"You stood up for me, Luffy! Thanks," Shanks said.

Luffy grabbed on to Shanks and sobbed as the serpent disappeared.

"Hey. You're safe!" Shanks smiled.

"I know," he sputtered, "but Shanks . . . your arm!"

Shanks held the boy with the only arm he had left.

"So what," he said. "A small price to pay for saving a mate."

*   *   *

It was days later when Shanks decided to set sail with his crew again, leaving young Luffy behind.

"So you're off?" Luffy asked, standing at the docks to see the pirates off.

"Sad to see us go?" Shanks asked with a smile.

"Yeah. But I won't ask to come with you! I'm becoming a pirate on my own! I wanna be top pirate! The best! I'm gonna be King of the Pirates!"

"Better than us, huh?" Shanks asked. "Well, then," he said as he lifted the straw hat from his head, "do me a favor. Keep this hat safe for me. This hat means a lot to me. So ya must promise to give it back someday. When you've become a great pirate."

Though Luffy could not have known, Shanks watched the boy as they sailed off to sea and thought, I hope that hat brings him all the luck of the seven seas.

CHAPTER THREE

Captain Buggy's Crew

Luffy sat cross-legged staring at his straw hat as he and Zolo continued to drift aimlessly in the open sea.

"Hey," Zolo called out. "You'll drop that hat again if you don't stop dreaming!"

"Thanks for saving it, Zolo," Luffy replied.

Zolo brushed off the gratitude and tried to bring Luffy's attention back to the present.

"I'm starving here! What are we gonna do?"

Luffy looked around. His eyes moved quickly from the water to the open sky.

"We'll eat!" Luffy declared. Then he pointed toward the sky. "That bird!"

Zolo smirked. "What are you talking about?"

Luffy smiled without answering. "Wait here!" he said as though there might be somewhere for Zolo to go.

"What?" Zolo answered. "Whadya mean?"

Luffy ignored Zolo and said, "Gum-Gum . . . Rocket!" The already lanky teenager nearly exploded out of himself. Zolo watched in amazement as Luffy stretched and stretched until his hands were wrapped snuggly around the crossbar of the mast. Then, Luffy used that leverage to catapult himself skyward until he was nothing more than a dot. His aim was perfect. He was headed right at the bird that was supposed to be lunch.

Unfortunately for Luffy, looks can be deceiving, especially from a distance. What had looked like a little bird from the boat was actually an enormous raptor. It didn't miss a beat when Luffy suddenly appeared alongside it high up in the sky. It simply opened its beak and Luffy was caught.

"Oh, boy," Luffy moaned.

"Lunch is served," Zolo said to himself, watching from far below, "and it's gonna be Luffy!"

"Help!" Luffy cried out. "A bird's got me!"

Zolo grabbed a paddle. "Curse you, Luffy, what are you doing?" He pulled hard on the paddle so that the little rowboat shot across the water, trailing the bird from below. He was so focused on tracking the bird that he didn't see the three heads bobbing up and down in the water directly in his path.

"Ahoy there! Ahoy there! Please help! We need to be rescued!" Three waterlogged pirates waved their arms and cried out for Zolo's attention.

When Zolo finally noticed them he said, "Grab on if you can! But I'm not stopping!" It was taking everything he had just to keep up with Luffy and his birdbrained transport. The pirates lunged for the boat and one by one dragged themselves up over the side.

"Well," said Zolo, glancing behind, "what do you know! You guys made it!"

The three pirates glared at Zolo. "That's right," they said, "we made it!"

If Zolo had taken the time to look at the scurrilous trio, he would have known that whatever they were about to announce was going to be trouble.

"We're pirates of Buggy the Clown!" they declared. "Now stop the ship, matey!"

If the pirates had taken the time to look at Zolo they might have known what he was about to announce too — with his instantly drawn sword.

It all happened so fast! Zolo! His sword! The pirates up and then . . . down.

The next words out of the pirates' mouths were, "We're sorry, Mister Pirate Hunter Zolo, sir, we didn't realize who you were." And then they began rowing the boat while Zolo rested against the stern, his sword laid casually in his lap.

"Thanks to you three," Zolo hissed at Buggy's pirates, "I lost sight of my friend. You better hope we catch up!"

"Yes, sir!" they called in unison and rowed ever harder.

"In the meantime," Zolo said, scanning the sky for signs of Luffy and the bird, "why don't you tell me what you were doing in the middle of the ocean."

"Well," offered up one, "we were out pirating for our cap'n —"

"— when we were pirated ourselves!" finished another.

"Aye," the third added, "and I'm sure word's gotten back by now that a *woman* hornswoggled us out of our treasure! Cap'n Buggy's gonna be as livid as a lobster!"

Zolo looked at the pirates with a furrowed brow. "Cap'n Buggy?"

"You never heard of Cap'n Buggy?" they asked in amazement.

"Doesn't ring a bell," said Zolo, unimpressed.

"That's cuz he's into honkin' horns!" the first pirate replied. "He's the most ferocious pirate in these parts! He has *powers* from a cursed fruit he ate. That clever lass may have stolen it from *us* but she won't get away with stealin' from Buggy or his army of pirates — that's for sure!"

Far off on shore, as if to prove the pirate's point, the red-haired girl named Nami who had swindled Buggy's pirates from their treasure was running for her life.

"I finally have it!" she declared to herself as she dashed through the streets of a deserted town, "the map of the Grand Line." Nami gripped a rolled paper in her hand as she tried to outrun the angry horde of pirates on her heels.

"Come back with our treasure map!" one pirate shouted as he nearly grabbed her.

"We mean it, missy!" shouted another as he drew his sword. "You'll be getting a knock-knock on your head you won't forget!"

Nami only ran faster as the pirates gasped and grunted behind her.

"We'll be getting the knock-knock if we don't get Buggy's map back," muttered another one of the pirates.

"True," gasped another. "He's got no sense of humor about these things."

In the middle of the deserted town, on the roof of one of the highest buildings, Buggy sat in his circus tent headquarters. His tone and his expression did nothing but prove his pirate's statement — no sense of humor.

"Cap'n Buggy," called one of his men, "our lookout reports something odd in the sky."

"Shoot it down," the angry clown pirate snarled.

In the next instant, Luffy was lost in a huge cloud of black smoke and then he was hurling through space, with earth coming ever nearer and in a hurry.

CHAPTER FOUR

Navigating Trouble

Nami looked up just as a strangely shaped shadow grew quickly at her feet.

"What the —?" called out a pirate behind her.

BOOM!

A swirl of smoke and dirt billowed up, blinding Nami and the pirates. Slowly, the dust began to settle.

"What happened?" Nami uttered.

A voice rose out of the rubble. "Wow! That was interesting . . . and I'm alive!"

Nami and the pirates watched in amazement as a tall young man stepped out of the smoke and rubble.

"I'm hungry!" Luffy suddenly exclaimed, overcome with a ravenous appetite.

But by then the pirates had gathered their wits and Nami could sense the sudden surprise had bought her as much time as it was going to. If she didn't escape now she'd lose the map. She glanced up the deserted street. She would need a little time to lose them around a corner or in a doorway. She turned back and studied Luffy, and at that moment, she knew what she would do.

"Boss!" she exclaimed, staring directly at Luffy. "You came back to rescue me!"

Luffy stared at Nami blankly. "Huh?"

Nami replied with a sweet smile.

Then Luffy said slowly, "You are . . .?"

The pirates began to grumble impatiently on the cobblestone street.

"I'll just let you take care of those guys by yourself!" Nami said to Luffy, already running down the street. "Later!"

"Stop her!" A pirate shouted. "She's getting away!"

"Forget her!" another responded. "We've got her boss right here!"

Luffy ignored the commotion. He could only focus on his empty belly. "Do you guys know where I can get some food?"

"You little vermin!" bellowed a muscle-bound pirate as he threw a punch at Luffy. "That map belongs to the fearsome pirate, Buggy the Clown!"

"Aaauuuggghhh!" wailed Luffy, half in pain and half in shock and surprise. But then he saw the real damage the blast had done. His straw hat was sailing up into the air. "My HAAATTT!" he cried out.

The thought of almost losing the hat for a second time in one day infuriated Luffy. Before it was even on its way back down, Luffy threw a fearsome punch and leveled the pirate.

"Take that!" he shouted as he held out his hand for the hat to land neatly upon it. "And don't touch the hat!"

"Scurvy bilge rat!" cried the remaining pirates as they charged toward Luffy, swords drawn.

High above, peaking over a rooftop's edge, Nami watched Luffy as the pirates descended upon him. "They're going to beat him up!" she whispered to herself.

Down below, Luffy prepared a deep blast.

"Gum . . . Gum . . . Blast!" Luffy exclaimed.

His arms sailed out in front of him at top speed and wiped out the rest of the pirates before they were even near him!

"Wow!" whispered Nami. *Pretty tough*, she thought. She sprang to her feet, a new idea brewing in her endlessly tricky mind. "Hey there!" she called out.

"Huh?" Luffy said from the quiet street below. He hadn't realized anyone was left standing.

"You beat those pirates by yourself!" she said as she leapt from a rooftop to a balcony with amazing ease.

Luffy watched the agile girl as she made her daring leaps. "Hey! Who are you?" he asked.

"Name's Nami," she replied, her red hair shining in the sun, a big smile on her face. "I specialize in robbing pirates! Wanna team up with me?! Yeah! Join my team!"

Luffy stared at her in amazement. He couldn't imagine a less likely offer. He *was* a pirate. Why would he rob himself?

"No. I really don't want to team up with you," he replied flatly. Before Nami could say another word, Luffy headed off down the street, leaving the band of Buggy's pirates strewn across the cobblestone.

"Hold on! Wait up! Hey!" cried Nami, making the final graceful leap from the balcony to the street. "I'm talking to you!" She chased after him until she was finally at his side.

But the grumbling in Luffy's stomach suddenly took control as he clutched his stomach and fell to his knees in hunger.

"Oh, yeah. I remember now . . . I need food."

Nami, never short on ideas, seized the moment. "No problem!" she declared. "Let's grab a bite to eat!"

"Wha — What did you say?" Luffy called out.

The notion of food wiped out any ill feelings he held for the girl who had so instantly betrayed him to Buggy's pirates.

Anything for food, he thought, and he followed her willingly.

CHAPTER FIVE

Taking Sides

Meanwhile . . .

Up on the highest roof of the deserted town at Cap'n Buggy's headquarters, things were not looking so good for Buggy's crew. As Buggy's skull-and-crossbones, clown-nosed flag flapped in the wind, the moment had come for the men to confess they'd not gotten Buggy his map.

"You still haven't caught that thief?!" the maniacal clown pirate growled. "This is inexcusable!"

An enormous, blond, bearded pirate quivered before Buggy, who sat perched in his thrown. "W — we're still searching . . . for her, Cap'n . . . Sir Buggy . . . Sir . . ."

Buggy showed no sign of softening. "How could you let the map of the Grand Line get stolen? Eh?!"

Buggy kept his tone even and calculated. This terrified the crew even more. He was going to blow, and the longer he waited, the worse it would be.

"And just when we were about to head there . . . and wreak havoc!?"

The pirate before Buggy clasped his hands together as the others tried to blend into one big undefined blob.

"The key to the map room . . ." the big pirate stumbled, searching for something — anything — to explain the situation to Buggy, "it got left in the lock and only the robber knows —"

Buggy cut the pirate off. "What did you say?!"

"I — I — I said, only the robber knows —" the pirate broke off in a whimper.

Suddenly Buggy was face-to-face — that is,

nose-to-nose — with the pirate. "What's that?" Buggy screamed, certain he was being mocked. "You think my nose looks like a *rubber nose*? You think it looks fake?"

"Sir," begged the pirate, "it was a mistake!"

"And now, it's a *steak*?" Buggy cried in anger.

Buggy was beginning to quiver, his anger growing by leaps and bounds. The pirate could not find the words to explain how he would never tease the cap'n about his bounteous — er — beautiful nose. It was nose use — er, no use! Once Buggy thought he'd been insulted, there was no turning back.

"You know you'll have to pay for that insult, don't you?" Buggy screeched.

"Cursed Fruit," shuddered another pirate, shaking in his boots.

"It gave Buggy amazing powers," cried another.

Suddenly the blond, muscled pirate was gasping for air. His huge body lifted off the ground and hung in the air. He kicked his legs and clutched at his throat. It was as if he were being strangled and yet no one was touching him.

"Help . . ." he croaked, ". . . can't . . . breathe . . ."

"What seems to be the problem," Buggy laughed. "You need some air?"

The pirate floated toward Buggy, who held his left hand clenched in a fist at his side. He spoke directly to the choking pirate. "No one insults my nose!"

"Please . . . spare . . . me . . ." gasped the pirate. "Sir . . . please . . . can't . . . breathe . . ."

Buggy didn't blink an eye. He simply opened up his clenched fist and the pirate fell in a heap on the ground, gasping for air.

"I'll spare you this time!" Buggy declared. "But don't think I'll be this generous next time!"

The rest of the crew looked on in terror as Buggy turned and walked determinedly back to his tent. "Now search every inch of this town and find me that map!" he shouted. "You understand?!"

The horror-struck crew leapt to attention and shouted in unison, "Sir! Yes, sir!"

* * *

In another part of town, Luffy sat on a bench at a wooden table in a clean, well-appointed home.

He had been eating for a while and was still packing it away as Nami looked on.

"This is delicious!" Luffy said, garbled between bites. "So you live in this big house all by yourself?"

Nami looked at him squarely. She spoke without emotion. "I don't live here. In fact, I don't even live in this town. Once Buggy and his pirates showed up, most everyone who lives here ran away."

"You're looting abandoned houses?" Luffy asked in amazement.

"Of course not," Nami shot back. "I rob pirates, not innocent people!"

Luffy continued to eat. Stolen or not, he had to have food. He swallowed and said, "But isn't a thief a thief?"

Nami's brow furrowed. "Look!" she exclaimed. "I've got my reasons." Clearly she was not going to say anything more about it. "But I will say," she continued, "I need a hundred million berries."

"That's a lot of money," Luffy said. "What do you need it for?"

"That's confidential," she said, turning away from him and looking more closely at the rolled-up scroll still clutched in her hand. "But with this map of the Grand Line I stole, I'm going to find more pirates to loot."

Luffy suddenly stopped chewing. "Map?" he exclaimed. "Are you a navigator?"

Nami turned back to him, a confident smile on her face. "Only the best in the whole wide world!"

Luffy leapt to his feet, "Nami! Why don't you join me and my crew and be *our* navigator!"

"Really?" she replied enthusiastically.

"Yes!" Luffy said. "You'll become a pirate just like us!"

As quickly as that, Nami's enthusiasm transformed to anger. "No!" she spat.

Luffy was confused.

"I didn't know you were a pirate," she snarled.

"Oh," Luffy smiled as he lifted his hat from his head. "I made a promise to the man who gave me this hat that I'd become King of the Pirates!"

Nami slammed the table with both hands. "If there's one thing I hate more than anything it's pirates!" she shouted. "What I like is money . . . and tangerines."

Luffy persisted. "Oh, come on. Be our navigator."

Nami walked to the window. "I said the answer's no!"

Luffy sat in defeat and continued to eat. "So the answer's no . . ." he mumbled.

Nami studied two men on the street below. She recognized them as Buggy's men. She listened carefully, trying to make out what they were saying.

"Did you find that thief?"

"No!"

"We have to get that map back!"

Nami stepped just out of view of the pirates and stole a glance at Luffy. She still had to figure a way out of town without getting grabbed by Buggy or his men. The clever wheels of her mind turned and in the next minute, it came to her. She walked back to Luffy with a renewed sweetness.

"You really do need a navigator so I'll join you under one condition," she said.

"Whatever you want!" Luffy declared with delight.

"I just want you to come with me to join Cap'n Buggy!"

* * *

Standing in the living room of the deserted house, Nami tied off a twisted mound of knots and stepped back to admire her work. Luffy's arms were strapped to his sides and bound with a dozen knots at his back. Nami held the end of the rope like a leash.

Still suspecting nothing but kindness from his newfound navigator, Luffy asked, "Why did you tie me up?"

Nami smiled another sweet smile and answered, "To show you I'm good with knots."

"Way cool!" Luffy exclaimed. "I've always enjoyed meeting new pirates, so let's go!"

* * *

At Buggy headquarters, Cap'n Buggy was busy instilling terror into another trio of pirates for their failure to capture the map thief.

"We're sorry," they cried to Buggy in his throne, nearly begging for their lives.

"Cap'n Buggy," called another voice, "it's the map thief, sir. She just walked through the door."

Buggy turned slowly to see Nami standing in wait with Luffy bound and leashed.

"What's going on?" Buggy growled, certain this must be a trick. "What's she up to?"

Nami walked across the open plaza with Luffy on the rope. She walked directly to Buggy and stood before his throne. She shoved the helpless Luffy forward so he fell to his knees before Buggy.

"Captain Buggy," Nami said coolly, "I've captured the real thief and I'm returning your map."

Luffy stared at Nami in disbelief. But she didn't give him so much as a glance. She was too focused on Buggy with a look of victory on her face.

CHAPTER SIX

Buggy Ball Battle

Captain Buggy studied the situation, searching for the trick. Finally, he said, "You're full of surprises. What made you change your mind?"

Nami was calm and collected. She didn't miss a beat when she said, "I had a really big fight with my boss. Whatya gonna do? Would it be alright if I team up with you instead?"

She handed Buggy the rolled-up scroll. Buggy's eyes clamped down in an angry squint. A nervous murmur flitted through the crowd of gathered pirates.

"Buggy's getting really angry now," one pirate said quietly.

"Power of the Cursed Fruit," said another, not far from where Luffy sat quiet.

Luffy's head was still spinning from Nami's betrayal but he couldn't help hear what the pirates were talking about.

"Cursed Fruit?" he repeated, amazed that he and Buggy had something in common.

Buggy's special glow began to radiate outward. The pirates braced themselves for the blast. But instead of rage, Buggy exploded into evil, hysterical laughter.

"You've got spunk!" he exclaimed to Nami. "Just having the guts to come back and ask me that . . . you'd make an outstanding member of my crew!" Buggy continued to laugh as Nami smiled sweetly.

Pirates are so gullible, she thought. As Buggy's men threw Luffy into a cage, Nami made a mental checklist of what she had to do: 1) grab Buggy's treasure, 2) take back the map, 3) make a quick getaway.

"Forget about joining my crew!" Luffy cried out from behind the thick steel bars of his cage. But nobody listened.

Buggy continued his mad cackling. "The map is mine again," he rejoiced. "What's your name?"

"Nami," she said confidently.

Buggy raised his arms up and turned to his crew. In a booming voice, he declared, "Let's hear it for Nami, the newest member of our crew! Hip hip, hooray!"

"Hooray!" cried the men. "To Buggy!"

A great party ensued. Some pirates ran amok while others performed acrobatic circus acts. Huge mounds of food and vats of drink came and went.

"Drink up!" Buggy exclaimed to Nami. "It's a special recipe! Grapefruit punch!"

Nami smiled. "It's delicious," she agreed without actually trying it. She kept a cool eye on the situation. The energy and excitement of the party continued to grow. *At this rate,* she thought, *they'll all*

pass out from acid indigestion and the treasure and map will be mine. Pirates are such easy prey!

On the edge of the festivities Luffy sat bound and caged. He quietly called upon his stretchy powers to reach through the raucous pirates to a table overflowing with food. He set his sights on a succulent roast beef.

"So close yet so far," he uttered as he stretched toward the meat. But before he could grab it, his arm snapped back and knocked him to the floor of his cage. "Hungry," he muttered.

Buggy roared with laughter.

"I'm feeling so good," he called out. "Tell you what! Load the special Buggy balls!" he commanded, and a deafening cheer rose up from the crowd.

At the far end of the party, an enormously heavy ball stamped with Buggy's clown-nosed skull and crossbones was loaded into the cannon.

"Buggy ball ready, Cap'n!"

Nami stood next to Buggy and watched with some concern.

"What's going on, Buggy?" she asked, trying to keep her tone casual.

"The time has come to demonstrate my power," he answered. "Watch this!"

Before another thought could pass through her head, a lit match was held to the cannon fuse and —

BOO-OOO-OOOM!! A blinding light matched a deafening roar as a section of the deserted town was leveled.

The explosion was so enormous, it was heard for miles and miles, even far off at sea where Zolo was still searching for Luffy.

* * *

Back at headquarters, Buggy was ecstatic. "Good show!" he cried. "Thanks to the Cursed Fruit and my Buggy ball, I'm going to rule the Grand Line! Right, Nami?"

Nami sputtered, "Of course." She couldn't believe the destruction Buggy had caused in the blink of an eye.

But Luffy heard only one thing: "rule the Grand Line." It pulled him out of his hunger-induced stupor.

"I'm the one who will rule the Grand Line 'cause I'm gonna be King of the Pirates!" he cried out.

Buggy's mood turned on a dime.

"You're a fool!" Nami shouted at Luffy. She was no fan of pirates but she didn't want to see Luffy get hurt and she knew Buggy would not respond calmly to those sorts of challenges.

"You're fed up with him, right?" Buggy bellowed at Nami.

Nami played along. "Yes! The hunger's gone to his head. He's delusional. He doesn't know how hard it is to be a good pirate. He's not a leader like you."

Side by side, Buggy and Nami stared at Luffy crunched in his cage.

"It's time you put your money where your mouth is, girlie," Buggy finally said. "Prove your loyalty and blow him up with this Buggy ball!"

Nami stammered, trying to figure a way out of this one.

"Now!" Buggy shouted.

Buggy rolled the cannon into position so that it stood about a hundred yards from Luffy, aimed directly at him.

Nami laughed nervously. "Why waste our time

with him?" she offered. "Let's go back to the party and have some more punch!"

But the party was coming to them. The empty corner of the plaza that had been deserted except for Buggy, Nami, and Luffy, in his cage, was filling with wound-up pirates.

"Show me you've got the guts to help me take over the world!" Buggy proclaimed as he handed her the matches.

"Blast him! Blast him!" the pirates shouted.

Nami searched herself for an answer. She knew the same fate awaited her if she didn't destroy Luffy, and yet, if she did do it, she would be no better than the scoundrels she despised. She stood frozen at the cannon, grasping for some way out. Luffy and Nami locked eyes at a distance as the pirates continued their obsessive chanting.

"Nami!" Buggy called out in a mocking tone, "don't be a party pooper!"

She began to tremble. Luffy watched in amazement as he realized she couldn't pull the trigger!

"You're shaking," he said from his cage. "You don't hate pirates as much as you say you do."

Anger mixed with her fear. "You think I don't hate pirates just because I'm not willing to blast someone like it's no big deal?"

Suddenly, an evil pirate grabbed the matches from her hand.

"Give me that! Quit stalling! Don't you know how to do it?" he teased as he lit a match. "You light it like so and then . . ." He held the lit match up and then lowered it toward the fuse. ". . . you touch it to the fuse —"

Nami couldn't allow it to happen. She moved with the grace of a ninja as she lifted an edge of her skirt to reveal four hidden sections of a collapsed defense pole. She assembled the pole with lightning speed, and with one swift swing, she slammed the match-happy pirate to the ground.

Silence descended as the crowd awaited Buggy's reaction.

"I couldn't help it," Nami said in her defense.

"You have betrayed me!" Buggy cried out.

"I'm sorry," Nami said, bowing.

But Buggy was through. "Cut it!" he screeched. "I'm not your fool!"

Luffy broke in, "Are you going to save me or what?"

"Don't be stupid," she yelled. "I just got carried away. I don't want to become a lowdown pirate like all of you! You pirates took someone very dear to me," she confessed. "I'll never become what I hate!"

Luffy listened carefully. He studied Nami's face and realized she had some sad secrets. Something terrible had happened to Nami and he wanted to know what it was. But that thought was swept away as he became aware of something a bit more urgent.

"The fuse is lit!" he screamed at the top of his lungs.

Nami flew into action.

"Stop her now!" Buggy commanded. Four pirates faced her with swords drawn. But with her stick and quick moves, Nami tangled the four pirates into a knot and raced for the burning fuse.

"Fire! Water! Fire! Water!" Luffy screamed.

Nami dove for the fuse and extinguished the flame with her bare hands.

"Aaaauuuggghhh!" she cried in anguish, smoke rising from her palms.

"Look out!" cried Luffy.

Nami knew the four pirates were about to attack her from behind. But she was overcome with the pain of the fire in her hands. She braced herself for the impact but it didn't come. Someone had stepped between them. Someone had come to her rescue.

"All of you against one of her?" the stranger said in a familiar voice.

Luffy laughed and shouted, "Zolo!"

Nami turned to see the strapping young pirate hunter holding off the four pirates. He threw them to the ground and turned to her.

"Are you alright, Nami?" he asked gently.

Stunned, she answered softly, "I'm fine."

"Hey, Zolo!" shouted Luffy. "Get me out of here!"

Everyone looked on in amazement. The pirates shifted nervously in the presence of the infamous pirate hunter. Nami stared, perplexed. Why would Zolo the Pirate Hunter partner up with Luffy the Pirate?

"So you're Zolo," Buggy said. "You're here to capture me and claim a huge reward!"

"Wrong," Zolo sneered. "I gave up pirate hunting. You mean nothing to me."

"Well, you mean something to me," Buggy cackled. "Capturing you would be a nice feather in my cap!"

Zolo and Buggy faced off, tension mounting. The pirates returned to chanting, "Buggy! Buggy!"

Zolo drew a collection of swords, holding one between his teeth. And then, suddenly, the two enemies were charging each other. Zolo, master swordsman, against Buggy and his cursed and mysterious Chop Chop powers.

In a matter of seconds, Zolo had sliced and diced Buggy into a dozen pieces. He lay scattered across the plaza. Luffy, Nami, and Zolo stood stunned.

"He wasn't much of an opponent after all," Zolo muttered.

"A total coward," Luffy added.

But then the laughter of the pirates around them drowned out their comments.

"I don't get it," Nami said. "Captain Buggy gets defeated and they're laughing?"

"What do you find so funny?" Zolo shouted, but in that instant, it all became clear. A bodiless hand holding a sword came sailing toward him from behind. He felt a piecing pain in his back and Zolo fell to his knees.

The Cursed Chop Chop!

"Chop! Chop! Chop!" Buggy's voice sailed through the air as the pieces of him began to reattach themselves to each other. "I'm a real cut-up, aren't I?" His horrible laughter rang out. "You can chop me but you can't stop me!"

"Buggy! Buggy!" chanted the pirates.

"He's a freak!" Luffy cried, still trapped in the cage and unable to help Zolo, who lay nearly motionless.

Buggy stood victorious over Zolo's bent body. Nami knew she had to do something. But what?

Suddenly, Luffy called out, "Stabbing someone in the back is a low blow! You got that, BIG NOSE?!"

The plaza went silent. The crowd waited to see just how Buggy would answer Luffy's loaded question. Without hesitation, he hurled a knife at Luffy. He was not prepared for Luffy's rubbery response. The knife bounced it right back at him.

"I'm gonna clobber you!" Luffy cried.

"This is the end of the road for all three of you!" raged Buggy.

But Luffy had another plan. He caught Zolo's squinted eye. In a split second, the two had come to a silent understanding. Zolo summoned up his remaining strength. With amazing precision, Luffy and Zolo went to work.

Zolo descended on Buggy with every sword he had. He sliced and diced but it didn't seem to matter against the Chop Chop curse.

"Three swords aren't better than one," Buggy laughed.

But Zolo wasn't listening. He was running toward the cannon. Before Buggy could stop him, Zolo had called upon the very last of his strength to upend the cannon. The nose of the cannon lifted straight up to the sky before falling down in the opposite direction it had been. Now it was loaded and aimed directly at Buggy!

The air filled with the terrified scream of Captain Buggy as he realized he was face to face with a Buggy ball.

Then the air filled with another sound.
BOO-OO-OO-OOM!!!

CHAPTER SEVEN

Furry Foes

The blast was so staggering, every pirate within a mile turned deaf and blind for at least as long as it took for the dust to settle. By then, Luffy, Nami, and Zolo had put some distance between themselves and whatever was left of Buggy and his crew.

They may have won for the moment, but Luffy was still trapped inside the concrete and steel cage and Zolo had battled to within an inch of his life.

Wounded and thoroughly exhausted, he seemed unable to stop himself. Stooped with pain, he dragged Luffy along in his cage.

"Zolo, you look beat up," Luffy said, concerned.

Sweat dripped down Zolo's face. "Just sit tight in your cage," he grunted, "and let me handle this mess we're in."

"Zolo," Nami said softly, her eyes open wide, "you should rest."

"I'm fine," he said as he winced in pain. "Except for my knee."

"Your knee looks fine to me," Luffy said, barely able to see from the confines of his cage.

"But it sounds awful," Nami said, cringing at the crunching sound coming from Zolo's knee. "You can't go on like this."

"I have to," Zolo cried out as he heaved the monstrously heavy cage onto his back, "and I will!"

Nami watched his heroics in amazement.

"We may have gotten ourselves into a mess," he spat. "But we're going to finish what we started."

Nami shook her head and spoke quietly to

herself, "These guys are something . . . for pirates, anyway."

* * *

Meanwhile, back in the rubble of Buggy's headquarters, Buggy was very much alive and plotting his revenge.

"How dare those sideshow phonies make a mockery of me!" His clownish eyes narrowed in anger. "I'll show them! Captain Buggy always gets the last laugh!" And he laughed long and hard.

"After all," he continued speaking as something in the distance began to take shape, "when you're looking to split a gut, there's one man you can always count on!"

Buggy laughed even harder as the distant shape approached and its details began to clarify. A pale-faced man with a snow-white beard and close-cropped head of hair approached. Curiously, his hair, or perhaps fur, continued onto his shoulders and chest. And if that weren't strange enough, the man-beast sat astride an enormous lion.

"Mohji, reporting! We're ready to maul Zolo!" the man-beast snarled.

Buggy giggled relentlessly. "Permission granted, Beast Breaker!"

*   *   *

Zolo stood with the cage raised above him. The massive weight threatened to crush him entirely. He hurled it ahead of him, each step getting them farther away from the enemy.

"Looks like," his breathing was heavy with only so much strength left in him, "we got away . . . for now."

He pushed the cage another few feet and finally came to a stop. "But before we strike back," Zolo forced out, "let's strategize."

Luffy smiled, turning to look Zolo in the face. But Zolo fell, facedown on the stones of the street. "And let's take a break," Zolo grunted.

Luffy was immediately distracted from Zolo's exhaustion by a small white dog sitting just beyond them, staring them down.

"Hey!" the caged Luffy called out. "Check it out! It's a dog!" Luffy rocked back and forth, forcing the cage to shimmy slowly across the cobblestone.

"Hey, pooch!" he called, but the dog didn't

move. Luffy pulled at his face, making strange sounds, hoping to urge a reaction from the pup but it only glared at him.

"This dog's acting stiff as a board," Luffy said to Zolo, who was propped up against a building wall.

"Yeah," Zolo said, eyes closed, "I know how he feels," and his head dropped.

"I wonder if he's real," Luffy said, incapable of leaving well enough alone. He stretched his arm past the cage bars and, with a single pointed finger, poked the dog between the eyes.

Faster than a flea bite, the dog attacked the cage. Even with the bars for protection, Luffy shouted in fear and pain. The dog was ferocious.

"Whoa!" screamed Luffy. "Heel! Fetch! Sit! Something! Just go away!"

Zolo bolted up, running on pure adrenaline. "Nice work, Luffy," he roared in frustration. "Can you tell he's real now?"

The dog finally backed away as, once again, all energy drained from Zolo's body.

"My break starts now," Zolo said, and the

heroic ex–pirate hunter fell again onto the cobble-stone just as Nami strode up.

Luffy looked at her from upside down where he lay in the cage still recovering from the dog attack.

"Nami!" he called, happy to see her. "Hi, navigator!"

"I don't think so," Nami said with a dismissive tone. "But here," she said and she tossed something small and metal onto the street. "This is in exchange for you saving me. I didn't want to owe you."

"Wow!" Luffy exclaimed. "It's the key! You stole the key to the cage! Thanks, Nami!"

Luffy grabbed for the key but before he could lay his rubbery hand on it, the cranky white pup swooped in and swallowed it down. That was the last straw. Now Luffy was ready to fight back.

"Give it back, you mangy mutt!" he cried as he grabbed the dog and the two battled it out with the bars between them.

RRRRR-ou-gh-gh!! RRRRR-ou-gh-gh!!
"Hey! Stop biting me!"
RRRRR-ou-gh-gh!! RRRRR-ou-gh-gh!!
"That's mine!"

RRRRR-ou-gh-gh!! RRRRR-ou-gh-gh!!

Nami watched, uncertain how to help. Zolo stared numbly, unable to move. But then, an unfamiliar voice rang out from the distance.

"Chouchou! What are you doing?" the voice cried.

The dog fell silent and so did everyone else. Nami turned first to see an old man in a brown jacket, green pants, and sandals watching from a distance. He had a flowing white beard and a piercing gaze.

"Don't attack them, Chouchou!" he instructed the dog. "At least, not until I hear what they're doing here . . . and it better be good."

After the unlikely trio introduced themselves to the old man, he moved quickly. Before Nami and Luffy realized it, he had carried Zolo away and disappeared into a house.

"Zolo!" Luffy cried as the old man returned alone.

"Your friend will be safe at my house," he said, his tone much softer than it had been. "I have access to the most advanced medical technology — a bed!"

Luffy eyed the man suspiciously.

"I'm going to help you," the old man said. "Any enemy of Buggy is a friend of mine!"

"Well, your dog doesn't treat us like friends," Nami said. Luffy nodded warily from behind his bars.

"He's not mine," the old spectacled man replied simply.

"He's not?" Nami confirmed.

The old man shook his head. "He belongs to the owner of that pet shop."

Nami looked up and realized they were standing in front of a deserted pet store. She turned back to the man.

"So who are you?" she asked.

"I am the mayor of the town — Mayor Boodle. I'm also a friend of the pet store owner. So it's my duty to feed the dog."

As he spoke he prepared and served a dish of food for the dog. He scratched the dog on the head after presenting the food. "Isn't that right, Chouchou," the man said suddenly speaking in baby talk, "my little snuggy wuggy puppy!"

Nami knelt down before the dog. "But where's the owner?" she asked gently.

"He passed on," the mayor said plainly as he returned the rest of the food to a shelf in the store and then closed the door behind him. "Some people think Chouchou sits here waiting for his owner to get back. But not me."

"No?" Nami replied, hoping the mayor would continue.

"Oh, no," he said. "Chouchou is far too smart for that. He knows very well his master is gone."

The little dog sat proudly, almost as if he understood they were talking about his dear departed master.

"So why does he just sit here, then?" Nami said, deeply curious.

"Because," the mayor said, eyeing Chouchou fondly, "this is all he has to remember his master by. It's his treasure."

Luffy and Nami understood all too well the importance of *treasure*. As they stared at the dog, they could imagine how important his master had been to him. Luffy felt like he could almost read the little dog's mind.

Gazing at the dog, Luffy imagined the dog's

cherished memories of his master. He could see them working together in the store. He could see the owner smiling proudly at Chouchou. He imagined them traveling together and enduring hardships side by side. They played together and shared meals together. And he could see the master bidding Chouchou a final farewell.

"Chouchou," the master would have said, "you're my best friend. But I have to go now . . . somewhere you can't follow. I love you, boy. And I know you'll always look after the shop for me!"

Luffy was lost in thought, feeling deeply sad for the little dog when — CRASH! BOOM! BOOM! He was yanked from his daydream as the earth shook beneath his cage.

"What's that?" Nami cried.

"We have to get out of here!" Boodle called out. "It's Mohji, the Beast Breaker!" The mayor grabbed Nami and they disappeared around a corner.

Luffy had never heard of Mohji but he knew trouble when he felt it rumbling. He knew he had to escape.

"How about it," he turned to the dog, "can I

get that key back?" With Zolo unconscious and Nami in the wind, it was up to Luffy to get himself free.

But it was too late. An enormous shadow extended out over Luffy's cage. He lifted his head until he was looking straight up.

He could see only one thing — the giant jaws of an enormous lion.

CHAPTER EIGHT

Battle of the Beast Breaker

The Beast Breaker breathed down Luffy's caged neck.

"Looks like your friends abandoned you! And after all that effort too!" Mohji teased.

"Hi," Luffy said brightly, seeming oblivious to the threat before him. "Who are you?" He was as unimpressed by the giant cat as he was the peculiar man riding atop it.

"You want introductions?" Mohji growled. "You handle your fear well, child."

"No," said Luffy candidly. "It's just that your costume doesn't scare me."

"Costume?" Mohji roared. "This is my hair!"

Luffy raised his eyebrows as he took a closer look. "How sad," he muttered.

Chouchou stood firm in the shadow of the monster. He crouched down, growling.

"Perhaps if I give you a small example of my powers you'll be wise enough to fear me!" Mohji dismounted the giant cat and stepped toward Chouchou with furry, clawed feet. "For there is no creature in the world who can't be controlled by Mohji, the breaker of beasts! Watch!"

Mohji reached out to Chouchou expecting to crush the little pup in a single move but Chouchou clamped down on the whole of Mohji's arm. Mohji jumped up and down, screaming in pain.

"Get rid of this mutt," he bellowed. "We're looking for Zolo."

That was like a magic word to the gigantic lion.

With one massive leap, the beast landed on Luffy's cage and shattered it to bits. Deafening roars filled the air as the lion lifted Luffy with a single swipe of its paw and hurled him backward into a row of buildings.

"Hey!" Luffy shouted, still stunned to be out of the cage, much less airborne. Then Luffy disappeared into the cloud of smoke and dust that rose up as he barreled into a group of buildings.

"Good boy," Mohji said to the lion. "How 'bout a little treat for such good work?"

Mohji moved toward Chouchou's pet store with a nasty smirk on his strange face. Chouchou stood firm at the doorway. As the lion and Mohji thundered toward him, he stood up growling and barking.

"Move, mutt!" Mohji cried. "My pet is hungry and we're going to get a snack from your pet store! You don't mind if we help ourselves, do you?"

Fueled with the memories of every wonderful moment he ever spent with his master, Chouchou braced himself to fight off the enormous enemies.

Down the street, Luffy shook himself off and got back to his feet. Around him lay the rubble of a half dozen houses that had been destroyed when he slammed through them.

"At least I'm out of that cage!" he crowed. "Now I'll show these clowns . . . and get Nami to be in my crew!"

Nami and Boodle appeared from their hiding spots. Nami's eyes were wide with wonder.

"How did you live through that?" she asked as Boodle nodded.

"What are you talking about?" Luffy asked casually, accustomed as he was to bouncing off things.

"Don't you think it's weird you crashed through all those buildings and don't have a mark on you?" Nami insisted.

Luffy stared blankly. "No," he said.

"What are you doing here, stranger?" Boodle asked with a renewed wariness. "What are you looking for?"

Luffy cocked his head like he'd never actually

thought about it. "I guess I'm here for the map to the Grand Line and to recruit Nami as the navigator for my crew! But first, I gotta make sure Zolo's okay!"

Luffy took off running, leaving Nami and Boodle far behind. He headed toward the pet store and Chouchou's battle where things were beginning to heat up.

The giant lion raised its enormous paw and swept it down toward Chouchou. The little dog was sent flying across the open road. But Chouchou would not surrender. It was as if he could hear his master's voice urging him on as he charged the massive enemy. This was his store. It was his job to protect it. He would not let his master down.

But by the time Luffy arrived, even Chouchou's great spirit could not defeat the enemy. The store lay in a pile of smoldering embers. Mohji was gone but had burned the store to the ground.

Luffy watched as the dog howled at the remains, giving voice to his broken heart. Luffy could barely stand to watch. He could feel himself filling with sadness for Chouchou. He didn't know what to do.

Before he could even reach out to Chouchou, he felt the ground begin to shake. Luffy spun around to see Mohji returning to the scene. He sat cross-legged, high atop his deadly massive lion.

"Don't tell me I didn't finish you off yet," Mohji snarled.

Luffy laughed at him. "Sorry, but I'm not that easy to get rid of!"

Mohji lunged off the lion and shouted, "Mighty beast! Sic 'im!"

In a flash, the lion was airborne, his enormous claws reaching out toward Luffy.

Luffy filled with all the sadness of Chouchou and all the rage for the destruction Mohji had brought. He looked directly at the lion and said, "Is that all you got?"

Mohji smirked with confidence. He was certain he had the battle won. He didn't know Luffy was about to call upon his special powers.

"Gum Gum Hammer!" called Luffy gleefully.

Before Mohji's frightened eyes, Luffy's arms twisted like a pretzel. The cyclone-spinning of Luffy's arms pulled the lion into a tornado. They flew through the air until Luffy raised the whirling dervish over his head and slammed it down into the street. Only the back half of the lion's body remained aboveground once the smoke and dust cleared.

"AAAUUUUGGGHHHH!!!" screamed Mohji. "What are you?"

"Just a guy who ate some Gum Gum fruit," replied Luffy.

Mohji began to tremble as he realized what he'd done. "You mean your powers are from a Cursed Fruit just like Captain Buggy's?"

Luffy nodded.

Mohji leapt back, hands in the air. "I owe you an apology," he spit out as fast as he could. Nervous sweat poured down his furry head.

"Too little too late, I'm afraid," said Luffy. "The damage has been done to that poor dog."

He looked to Chouchou, who barked at him with a new respect.

"And now damage will have to be done to you," Luffy said.

As Mohji wept in fear and Chouchou watched stoically, Luffy stretched his arms along a great length of the village road until his hands wrapped around Mohji's neck and wrenched him forward. With one more massive rubber Gum Gum blast, Luffy laid out the Beast Breaker on the street, defeated.

CHAPTER NINE

Boodle's Revenge

Hours later, Nami and Boodle stood before the remains of the pet store. The little dog sat quietly, head lowered.

"Poor Chouchou," whispered Nami. "He had one thing he loved in this world and now it's gone. Lousy pirates! They do as they please and don't care who gets hurt along the way."

As she spoke quietly to herself, Luffy appeared from around a street corner. Nami saw him and sneered. "Luffy is no exception," she said. Then she turned to look him straight in the face.

"I thought for sure you'd be eaten by that lion," she said in mock amazement. Then with a hiss, she added, "But I guess that was just wishful thinking!"

Luffy stared at her, a sadness etched across his face.

Nami pushed ahead, "I should stop you now before you get a pirate crew and wreck some poor town!"

Boodle grabbed her by the shoulders. "Take it easy!" he insisted.

Luffy hung his head and walked over to the little dog.

"Hey, Chouchou," Luffy said gently. "Here's a little present." The pirate boy set a box of pet food down before the dog. The box was crumpled and ripped as it had been grabbed from the jaws of Mohji's lion but it was familiar to the dog.

"I know it doesn't look like much but I'm afraid it's all that's left of your shop." He sat down next to Chouchou, offering up his company and comfort.

Nami watched in wide-eyed disbelief. She

stuttered slightly when she finally spoke. "Luffy fought against the big beast . . . for the dog?" she gasped. It went against everything she had assumed about Luffy.

Chouchou gave a small yip, then picked up the box in his mouth before walking away from the people.

"I didn't see it," Luffy said kindly, "but I bet you put up a good fight against that lion, huh, Chouchou? You must be exhausted."

Chouchou stopped walking and set the box down so that he could turn back to Luffy and offer up a small yip of thanks.

Luffy smiled and responded, "Thanks! You too! See ya!"

Nami smiled, in spite of herself.

* * *

Back at Buggy's tent, Mohji crouched before the captain. He was the picture of a broken Beast Breaker.

"What do you mean *beaten*?" Buggy snarled.

"I — I — I'm sorry, Cap'n," Mohji stammered. "He was just too strong."

"Oh, please," Buggy snapped, "how strong could this Zolo fellow be?"

"No!" Mohji shuddered. "It was a boy! With a straw hat . . ."

Buggy's eyes narrowed as he crouched down in anger. "What? A boy in a straw hat? What do you take me for?"

But his rage couldn't do any more damage to Mohji. The lion man fell over in defeat mumbling, "And he's rubber too!"

"I've heard enough!" erupted Buggy. "Ready the special Buggy balls!"

Back in the village, Nami begged forgiveness from Luffy, who still sat on the street where Chouchou had been.

"I shouldn't have yelled at you," she said to Luffy.

Luffy looked up at her and his face gave way to his trademark grin. "That's okay. I'm sure you had your reasons. I say we forget all about it!"

Just as Nami and Luffy were about to move on, Boodle stopped them.

"Luffy!" the old mayor called out, his voice

laced with a passionate rage. "You and Chouchou have shown more guts for this town in one day than I have in all the time I've been mayor. Your courage has been a wake-up call for me to rise and shine!"

Luffy stood, shocked.

Nami reached out to the mayor. "Mayor, hold on!"

But Boodle wouldn't stop. He stood tall and looked at the old buildings all around him. "Forty years ago, this town was barren land. But we culti-vated the soil, plowed the field, opened up shops! We built a civilization! And we did it with our own blood, sweat, and tears! This town and its people are my treasures and I'm not going to let Buggy and his crew plunder them anymore!"

As if Buggy had been listening for the perfect moment to launch his attack, a dreadful whistling noise filled the air and then —

BOO-OO-OO-OOM!!!

Everything exploded in lightning flashes and furious noise. Buggy was out to blow the whole town to smithereens!

Boodle was the first to realize how close to

them the Buggy ball had landed. The dust had only begun to settle when he pointed to a pile of rubble and cried out, "That was my house!"

Luffy leapt up. "That's where Zolo was!"

Boodle and Nami stared at the smoking wreckage. "There's no way he could have survived," Boodle said.

But Luffy knew better. "Zolo!" he called out. "Are you alive?"

From out of the dust came the familiar voice, "Far as I can tell . . ."

Luffy's laugh filled the thick air as Zolo became visible through the smoke. He sat in the rubble, his green-haired head in his hands.

"That's some alarm clock!" he muttered.

Nami looked on in wonder. "How could you have survived?"

"He's alive!" cheered Luffy.

But Boodle's rage had only grown.

"I won't take this anymore!" he said, fists clenched. "Pirate bullies! I won't let them wreck forty years of hard work! I won't take this sitting down."

Nami could sense the danger in Boodle's anger.

"Mayor, wait, please!" she begged, using all her might to keep him from rushing off to Buggy's headquarters.

"You agree, don't you, boy?" the mayor called to Luffy.

"Sounds good to me!" Luffy said, always itching for a pirate adventure.

Nami turned to him in frustration. "Getting yourself hurt won't accomplish anything!"

The mayor broke away from her and hurried toward Buggy's headquarters. "I know what chances I'm taking," he called out.

Zolo sat quietly as the mayor disappeared in search of justice.

"He's not using his head," Nami cried.

"Nope," Luffy agreed. "He's using his heart."

Zolo lifted his head and finally spoke, "Tough choice. Headache or heartache."

"The mayor's a good man," Luffy said. "I'm going to protect him."

"Right," said Zolo, swords already gathered. "Let's go!"

"Where are you going?" Nami insisted. "You're hurt!"

"I'm more worried about my reputation than my wounds right now," he said as he tied a bandanna around his forehead. "I gotta settle a score!"

"Yeah!" said Luffy. "And that will let us steal back the map of the Grand Line! Join us, Nami! You like treasure!"

Nami's brow furrowed as she slapped away Luffy's outstretched hand. "No way!" she replied. "I'm not becoming a pirate!" But then she laughed. "But who says we can't be partners for a common cause?"

Luffy laughed too and the trio headed off to rescue the mayor.

CHAPTER TEN

Circus Tricks

"I want you gone, Buggy the Clown!" cried the mayor from the street below Buggy's rooftop headquarters. He stood panting and irate. He held a single spear as protection.

The unexpected command interrupted Buggy just as he was ordering another Buggy ball to be fired into the middle of the town. Buggy and his crew leaned over the edge and looked down on the mayor.

"This town is my one treasure in the world," cried the mayor, "and I won't just sit by and watch you ruin it!"

Buggy and his crew laughed at the mayor.

"You senile old fool!" screeched Buggy. "Treasure is made up of gold and silver! This town is made up of good-for-nothing losers like you!"

Boodle raged on, "Come down and face me!"

Buggy's laughter grew louder and crueler. "You dare to cast orders at me, old man? You're talking to the future ruler of the Grand Line! The soon to be conqueror of One Piece! And, thanks to the Cursed Fruit I ate, the only pirate captain who can reach out and touch . . . anyone!"

His maniacal laughter reached new heights as he called upon his special powers. From a far distance, many stories up from Boodle, he clenched his fist and Boodle rose into the air, choking.

"I . . . must . . . protect the town," the mayor gasped. "I must . . . stop . . . you!"

"Say good-bye," Buggy said with an evil giggle.

The mayor's lungs felt as though they might

explode as the last bits of air left him. But then, suddenly, there was a relief. The mayor fell to his knees as renewed life filled his body. The grip around his neck disappeared. As he caught his breath, he looked up to see Luffy standing before him, holding off Buggy's evil hand.

"It's the straw-hat kid!" cried Buggy.

"That's right!" Luffy announced. "And I'm back to clobber you just like I promised!"

"Unhand me!" Buggy insisted, struggling to regain the upper hand.

Luffy laughed as the mayor tried desperately to regain his strength and continue his battle.

"You have a lot of nerve coming back here!" shouted Buggy. "Are you mad? Or do you just enjoy feeling pain?"

Nami watched impatiently. There was no doubt they were headed for another pirate altercation. She turned to Zolo and said, "You guys have fun fighting but I'm here for the map and the treasure."

"So you've said," Zolo said, rolling his eyes at Nami as she, once again, threatened to leave them behind.

The mayor's desperate cry interrupted them.

"This is my town, you got that!" he demanded. "I'm going to protect it!" Still coughing, he turned on Zolo and Luffy. "I don't need a bunch of young whippersnappers fighting my battles for me!"

The old man reached for his walking stick and pulled himself up to stand.

"Don't interfere!" he said to Luffy. But Luffy extended his rubber arms forcefully and pushed the mayor so that he smashed into a wall and slid down to the ground, unconscious.

Zolo studied the scene but made no remark. Nami was aghast.

"Whose side are you on?" she cried. "Why did you do that?"

"Simple," smiled Luffy. "He was in the way."

Zolo stepped up as Nami searched for something to say.

"Good thinking," said Zolo. "He never would have survived against the clown creep. He's a lot safer unconscious."

Nami threw up her hands in disugust. "You're

too reckless," she shouted. "Did you have to knock him out cold?!"

But Luffy's attention had moved to the battle at hand.

"Watch this!" he announced. "Hey! Big nose!"

An audible gasp rose up from the pirates around Buggy. Then a silence gripped the crowd as they waited for their captain to explode.

"You shouldn't have said that," Nami whispered.

"READY THE CANNON!" Buggy's voice rang out. "SPECIAL BUGGY BALLS! FIRE!!!"

Zolo and Nami watched in terror as the cannon aimed directly at Luffy. But Luffy stood his ground and watched as a match touched the fuse.

"Luffy!" Zolo gasped. "You're gonna get hit!"

"That's the idea," Luffy said with a smile.

"Say your prayers," Buggy screeched.

"I can take it!" Luffy said, bracing himself. "Gum Gum Balloon!"

Gritting his teeth, Luffy expanded himself into an enormous rubber orb. Nami and the pirate crew watched in shock and horror as the Buggy ball sailed into the middle of Luffy and disappeared in the rubbery mass only to reemerge, sailing back in the opposite direction.

Buggy watched in desperation and anger. "He took a direct hit!" he screamed. "And now . . . he's bouncing it back!"

Buggy and his crew screamed in terror and ran for cover as the dreaded Buggy ball came sailing back in their direction.

BOO-OOO-OOOOM!

Nami and Zolo ran to Luffy.

"Next time, clue us in," Zolo said, relieved.

Nami stared at him with brows furrowed. "I knew there was something strange about you! You should have been blown to bits! What kind of human being does these things? First you pile drive a lion and now this. How do you inflate yourself like a balloon?"

Luffy laughed. "A Gum Gum balloon," he stated in explanation.

But Nami didn't understand. "I don't care if it's a dumb-dumb balloon, I just want to know how you did it!"

But Buggy didn't allow an answer.

"You've got some nerve, Straw Hat. But your little balloon trick won't save you from my wrath!"

Just then, Mohji appeared from inside head-quarters. When he caught sight of Luffy he let go a terrified yelp.

"That's him! The Straw Hat Kid!" he screeched. "He has special powers like you, Cap'n! He ate the Cursed Fruit and now he's made of rubber!"

"Rubber?" Nami repeated.

Luffy smiled at her and pulled his cheek far away from his face as friendly proof.

Up on the rooftop, Buggy had called on yet another member of his weird pirate circus troop.

A trim little pirate in tights stepped to the roof's edge. "Is it time to take revenge, sir?" he asked Buggy.

"Yes!" Buggy cackled. "Let the greatest show on earth begin!"

The little pirate revealed an evil smile.

"Ladies and gentlemen," exclaimed Buggy, "Cabaji the acrobat!"

From below, Luffy, Nami, and Zolo watched

as the acrobat threw himself into a series of impossible positions. But then, suddenly, Cabaji was standing before Luffy.

"For my first trick," he announced, "I'll slice you to mincemeat."

Nami screamed, "Get out of the way!"

Zolo leapt into action. "If it's a sword duel you want, I'm your man."

"It will be my honor to cut you down!" Cabaji hissed.

Luffy and Nami watched as Zolo battled the nasty acrobat who had more than handstands in his arsenal. He spit fire, blew steam, and sliced and diced. And he focused all his evil attention on Zolo's injuries.

"That's not fair!" Nami cried.

Zolo was on the ground, nearly defeated.

"You're supposed to be a scary pirate hunter!" Cabaji laughed. "But look at you writhing on the ground!"

"Zolo's hurt bad!" Nami cried to Luffy. "How can you just stand there?"

But Zolo lifted his head. "You're annoying," he

spat. "Picking on an injured man. Well, go ahead. Give it your best shot!"

Cabaji blasted Zolo again and reopened the wound on his back. Zolo stood unflinching.

"Are my injuries enough of a handicap for you?" Zolo tested. "You'd better hope so 'cause now you're going to see some real swordplay!"

Nami turned away, scared and disgusted. "I've seen enough! Win or lose, I don't care!" she lied. "I've got a date with a treasure chest," she said quietly and then she slipped away from view.

Just then, Cabaji shouted, "Prepare for the greatest of my tricks — The Dance of a Thousand Tumultuous Tops!"

Suddenly the air filled with deadly slicing tops. Zolo's swords became a blur as he slashed them through the air, fending off the tops. But that was just the beginning of Cabaji's circus act. He attacked with everything from piercing rocks to blazing fireworks. Zolo defended but could do nothing more until finally he held up his sword.

"I'm tired," he said, panting, "I've had enough."

"Tired?" laughed Cabaji. "Bad night's sleep?"

"You've got it wrong," Zolo growled. "I'm tired of your stupid circus tricks."

Cabaji's anger flashed. He roared, "Then no more circus tricks! Play time is over!"

The two stood face-to-face, swords drawn. The tiniest of grins flashed across Zolo's face. This was the kind of battle he knew how to fight.

"Oni," said Zolo.

"*En garde*!" replied Cabaji.

"Giri!" answered Zolo, and with blinding speed he descended on Cabaji. He was masterful. Not a single movement was wasted. Zolo proved his reputation. Cabaji was writhing on the ground, screaming in pain before Buggy or anyone else could swoop in to help him.

"Cabaji," Buggy cried.

"Beaten by common thieves," Cabaji gasped.

"Not just any thieves," Zolo declared, "we're pirates!"

CHAPTER ELEVEN

Cursed Fruit vs. Cursed Fruit

"I'll take it from here," Luffy said as Zolo sat down in exhaustion next to Boodle, who only groaned in his sleep.

Luffy reached a rubbery arm toward Buggy, who had descended with his men to claim Cabaji.

"Hand over the map to the Grand Line!" Luffy ordered.

"So that's what you're after," cackled Buggy. "A bunch of lily-livered pirates like you won't last a day on the Grand Line! What are you going to do when you get there, Straw Hat?"

"Be King of the Pirates!" Luffy declared without hesitation.

"Ha!" laughed Buggy. "Then what am I? Emperor?"

"Let's go," Luffy said to Zolo, who snored back. "I'm getting bored."

"I can fix that," Buggy replied. "You'll soon regret your words, Rubber Boy!" Then the clown pirate studied Luffy long and hard. "You and your stupid hat," he spat, "remind me of . . . *him*. That insolent dog . . . with the red hair!"

Luffy's jaw dropped. "Are you talking about Shanks?" he asked in amazement. "Do you know where he is?"

"Maybe, maybe not," answered Buggy, realizing he'd hit upon a vulnerable spot in Luffy.

"What are you talking about?" Luffy insisted,

furious that this clown would keep such valuable information from him.

"We're mortal enemies," Buggy replied. "You won't get any information out of me without a fight!"

Luffy took him at his word, shouting, "Gum Gum FIST!" His clenched hand went flying toward Buggy.

But Buggy called upon his own powers, "Chop Chop BUZZSAW!"

Before Luffy could respond, the edge of a blade nicked his head. He grabbed for his hat and stopped in his tracks. Buggy watched in disbelief.

"Did the widdle baby get a boo-boo?" Buggy mocked.

"You nicked my hat," Luffy answered. "Now I'm angry. This isn't just any old hat. It's my treasure and nobody damages it!" Luffy was flooded by his memories of Shanks as he stared at the ripped hat.

"You call this beat-up thing a treasure?" Buggy scoffed.

"It's Shanks' and I promised I'd give it back," he shouted, a rage building.

"Shanks!?" Buggy screamed, his evil eyes bulging. "I knew the hat looked familiar! He always wore it! Never took it off!"

Luffy stared at Buggy in disbelief. "You sailed with him?"

"We were shipmates," Buggy hissed. "Comrades."

"Shanks is a great man. He'd never be a comrade to a clown like you."

Buggy laughed, mocking Luffy's sincerity. "I'll curse him as long as I live," Buggy said. "He stole a great treasure from me."

"Don't you ever mention Shanks and yourself in the same breath again," Luffy threatened, and he and Buggy stared each other down.

Luffy gripped his hat, feeling the rough tear with his thumb. Never had he felt so much anger for one person as he did for Buggy in that moment. He suddenly knew this would not be the last time he battled this pirate clown. But he also knew he would win because anyone who vowed to ruin Shanks would have to go through him, and he would never let Shanks down.

He knew something else too. He would be the greatest pirate of all time. He would be the Pirate King. Shanks had told him so.